# THE HOUSE
# AMONG THE LAURELS

BY

WILLIAM HOPE HODGSON

**British Library Cataloguing-in-Publication Data**
A catalogue record for this book is available from the
British Library

# CONTENTS

# WILLIAM HOPE HODGSON

William Hope Hodgson was born in Essex, England in 1877. He began a four-year apprenticeship as a cabin boy at the age of fourteen, and spent most of his teens at sea. In 1899, having returned to Blackburn, England, he became a well-known bodybuilder, and his first writing endeavours were essays on the subject of fitness and health. He turned his attention to fiction during the early part of the 20th century, and in 1904 published his first short story, 'The Goddess of Death'. Over the next few years, his fiction spread to the American market, where his 'Sargasso Sea stories' were well-received. Hodgson wrote prolifically for the rest of his life, and is best-known nowadays for two novels – *The House on the Borderland* (1908) and *The Night Land* (1912) – and the much-anthologised stories 'The Whistling Room', 'The Voice in the Night' and 'The Shamraken Homeward-Bounder'. Hodgson was killed by an artillery shell at Ypres in April of 1918.

# THE HOUSE AMONG THE LAURELS

*William Hope Hodgson*

'This is a curious yarn that I am going to tell you,' said Carnacki, as after a quiet little dinner we made ourselves comfortable in his cosy dining-room.

'I have just got back from the West of Ireland,' he continued. 'Wentworth, a friend of mine, has lately had rather an unexpected legacy, in the shape of a large estate and manor, about a mile and a half outside of the village of Korunton. The place is named Gannington Manor, and has been empty a great number of years; as you will find is so often the case with houses reputed to be haunted.

'It seems that when Wentworth went over to take possession, he found the place in very poor repair, and the estate totally uncared for, and, as I know, looking very desolate and lonesome generally. He went through the big house by himself, and he admitted to me that it had an uncomfortable feeling about it; but, of course, that might be nothing more than the natural dismalness of a big, empty house, which has been long uninhabited, and through which one is wandering alone.

'When he had finished his look round, he went down to the village, meaning to see the one-time Agent of the Estate, and arrange for someone to go in as caretaker. The Agent, who proved, by the way, to be a Scotsman, was very willing to take up the management of the Estate once more; but he assured Wentworth that they would get no one to go in as caretaker; and that his—the Agent's—advice was to have the house pulled down, and a new one built.

'This, naturally, astonished my friend, and, as they went down to the village, he managed to get a kind of explanation from the man. It seems that there had always been curious stories told about the place, which in the early days was called Landru Castle, and that within the last seven years there had been two extraordinary deaths there. In each case they had been tramps, who were ignorant of the reputation of the house, and had probably thought the big empty place suitable for a night's free lodging. There had been absolutely no signs of violence to indicate the method by which death was caused, and on each occasion the body had been found in the great entrance hall.

'By this time they had reached the inn where Wentworth had put up, and he told the Agent that he would prove that it was all rubbish about the haunting, by staying a night or two in the Manor himself. The death of the tramps was certainly curious; but did not prove that any supernatural agency had been at work. They were but isolated accidents, spread over a large number of years by the memory of the villagers, which was natural enough in a little place like Korunton. Tramps had to die some time, and in some place, and it proved nothing that two, out of possibly hundreds who had slept in the empty house, had happened to take the opportunity to die under its shelter.

'But the Agent took his remark very seriously, and both he and Dennis, the Landlord of the inn, tried their best to persuade him not to go. For his "sowl's sake", Irish Dennis begged him to do no such thing; and because of his "life's sake", the Scotsman was equally in earnest.

'It was late afternoon at the time, and as Wentworth told me, it was warm and bright, and it seemed such utter rot to hear those two talking seriously about the Impossible. He felt full of pluck, and he made up his mind he would smash the story of the haunting, at once, by staying that very night in the Manor. He made this quite clear to them, and told them that it would be more to the point and to their credit, if they offered to come up along with him, and keep him company. But poor old Dennis was quite shocked, I believe, at the suggestion; and though Tabbit, the Agent, took it more quietly, he was very solemn about it.

'It appears that Wentworth did go; though, as he said to me, when the evening began to come on, it seemed a very different sort of thing to tackle.

'A whole crowd of the villagers assembled to see him off; for by this time they all knew of his intention. Wentworth had his gun with him, and a big packet of candles; and he made it clear to them all that it would not be wise for anyone to play any tricks; as he intended to shoot "at sight". And then, you know, he got a hint of how serious they considered the whole thing; for one of them came up to him, leading a great bull-mastiff, and offered it to him, to take to keep him company. Wentworth patted his gun; but the old man who owned the dog, shook his head and explained that the brute might warn him in sufficient time for him to get away from the castle. For it was obvious that he did not consider the gun would prove of any use.

'Wentworth took the dog, and thanked the man. He told me that, already, he was beginning to wish that he had not said definitely that he would go; but, as it was, he was simply forced to. He went through the crowd of men, and found suddenly that they had all turned in a body and were keeping him company. They stayed with him all the way to the Manor, and then went right over the whole place with him.

'It was still daylight when this was finished, though turning to dusk; and, for a little, the men stood about, hesitating, as if they felt ashamed to go away and leave Wentworth there all alone. He told me that, by this time, he would gladly have given fifty pounds to be going back with them. And then, abruptly, an idea came to him. He suggested that they should stay with him, and keep him company through the night. For a time they refused, and tried to persuade him to go back with them; but finally he made a proposition that got home to them all. He planned that they should all go back to the inn, and there get a couple of dozen bottles of whisky, a donkey-load of turf and wood and some more candles. Then they would come back, and make a great fire in the big fireplace, light all the candles, and put them round the place, open the whisky and make a night of it. And, by Jove! he got them to agree.

'They set off back, and were soon at the inn, and there, whilst the donkey was being loaded, and the candles and whisky distributed, Dennis was doing his best to keep Wentworth from going back; but he was a sensible man in his way; for when he found that it was no use, he stopped. I believe, he did not want to frighten the others from accompanying Wentworth.

' "I tell ye, sorr," he told him, " 'tis no use at all at all thryin' to reclaim ther castle. 'Tis curst with innocent blood, an' ye'll be betther pullin' it down, an' buildin' a fine new wan. But if ye be intendin' to shtay this night, kape the big dhoor open whide, an' watch for the bhlood-dhrip. If so much as a single dhrip falls, don't shtay though all the gold in the worrld was offered ye."

'Wentworth asked him what he meant by the blood-drip.

' "Shure," he said, " 'tis the bhlood av thim as ould Black Mick, 'way back in the ould days, kilt in their shlape. 'Twas a feud as he pretendid to patch up, an' he invited thim— the O'Haras they was—sivinty av thim. An' he fed thim, an' shpoke soft to thim, an' thim thrustin' him, shtayed to shlape with him. Thin, he an' thim with him, stharted in an' mhurdered thim wan an' all as they slep'. 'Tis from me father's grandfather ye have the sthory. An' sence thin 'tis death to any, so they say, to pass the night in the castle whin the bhlood-drip comes. 'Twill put out candle an' fire, an' thin in the darkness the Virgin Herself would be powerless to protect ye."

'Wentworth told me he laughed at this; chiefly because, as he put it: One always must laugh at that sort of yarn, however it makes you feel inside. He asked old Dennis whether he expected him to believe it.

' "Yes, Sorr," said Dennis, "I do mane ye to b'lieve it; an', please God, if ye'll b'lieve, ye may be back safe befor' mornin'." The man's serious simplicity took hold of Wentworth, and he held out his hand. But, for all that, he went; and I must admire his pluck.

'There were now about forty men, and when they got back to the Manor—or castle as the villagers always call it—they were not long in getting a big fire going, and lighted candles all round the great hall. They had all brought sticks; so that they would have been a pretty formidable lot to tackle by anything simply physical; and, of course, Wentworth had his gun. He kept the whisky in his own charge; for he intended to keep them sober; but he gave them a good strong tot all round first, so as to make things cheerful; and to get them yarning. If you once let a crowd of men like that grow silent, they begin to think, and then to fancy things.

'The big entrance door had been left wide open, by his orders; which shows that he had taken some notice of Dennis. It was a quiet night, so this did not matter, for the lights kept steady, and all went on in a jolly sort of fashion for about three hours. He had opened a second lot of bottles, and everyone was feeling cheerful; so much so that one of the men called out aloud to the ghosts to come out and show themselves. And then, you know, a very extraordinary thing happened; for the ponderous main door swung quietly and steadily to, as if pushed by an invisible hand, and shut with a sharp click.

'Wentworth stared, feeling suddenly rather chilly. Then he remembered the men, and looked round at them. Several had ceased their talk, and were staring in a frightened way at the big door; but the greater number had never noticed, and were talking and yarning. He reached for his gun, and the following instant the great bull-mastiff set up a tremendous barking, which drew the attention of the whole company.

'The hall I should tell you is oblong. The south wall is all windows; but the north and the east have rows of doors leading into the house, while the west wall is occupied by the great entrance. The rows of doors leading into the house were all closed, and it was towards one of these in the north wall that the big dog ran; yet he would not go very close; and suddenly the door began to move slowly open, until the blackness of the passage beyond was shown. The dog came back among the men, whimpering, and for perhaps a minute there was an absolute silence.

'Then Wentworth went out from the men a little, and aimed his gun at the doorway.

' "Whoever is there, come out, or I shall fire," he shouted; but nothing came, and he blazed both barrels into the dark. As though the report had been a signal, all the doors along the north and east walls moved slowly open, and Wentworth and his men were staring, frightened, into the black shapes of the empty doorways.

'Wentworth loaded his gun quickly, and called to the dog; but the brute was burrowing away in among the men; and this fear on the dog's part frightened Wentworth more, he told me, than anything. Then something else happened. Three of the candles over in the corner of the hall went out; and immediately about half a dozen in different parts of the place. More candles were put out, and the hall had become quite dark in the corners.

'The men were all standing now, holding their clubs, and crowded together. And no one said a word. Wentworth told me he felt positively ill with fright. I know the feeling. Then, suddenly, something splashed on to the back of his left hand. He lifted it, and looked. It was covered with a great splash of red that dripped through his fingers. An old Irishman near to him, saw it, and croaked out in a quavering voice: "The bhlood-dhrip!" When the old man called out, they all looked, and in the same instant others felt it upon them. There was frightened cries of: "The bhlood-dhrip! The bhlood-dhrip!" And then, about a dozen candles went out simultaneously, and the hall was suddenly almost dark. The dog let out a great, mournful howl, and there was a horrible little silence, with everyone standing rigid. Then the tension broke, and there was a mad rush for the main door. They wrenched it open, and tumbled out into the dark; but something slammed it with a crash after them, and shut the dog in; for Wentworth heard it howling as they raced down the drive. Yet no one had the pluck to go back to let it out, which does not surprise me.

'Wentworth sent for me the following day. He had heard of me in connection with that Steeple Monster Case. I arrived by the night mail, and put up with him at the inn. The next day we went up to the old manor, which certainly lies in rather a wilderness; though what struck me most was the extraordinary number of laurel bushes about the house. The place was smothered with them; so that the house seemed to be growing up out of a sea of green laurel. These, and the grim, ancient look of the old building, made the place look a bit dank and ghostly, even by daylight.

'The hall was a big place, and well lit by daylight; for which I was not sorry. You see, I had been rather wound-up by Wentworth's yarn. We found one rather funny thing, and that was the great bull-mastiff, lying stiff with its neck broken. This made me feel very serious; for it showed that whether the cause was supernatural or not, there was present in the house some force dangerous to life.

'Later, whilst Wentworth stood guard with his shot-gun, I made an examination of the hall. The bottles and mugs from which the men had drunk their whisky were scattered about; and all over the place were the candles, stuck upright in their own grease. But in that somewhat brief and general search, I found nothing; and decided to begin my usual exact examination of every square foot of the place—not only of the hall, in this case, but of the whole interior of the castle.

'I spent three uncomfortable weeks, searching; but without result of any kind. And, you know, the care I take at this period is extreme; for I have solved hundreds of cases of so-called "hauntings" at this early stage, simply by the most minute investigation, and the keeping of a perfectly open mind. But, as I have said, I found nothing. During the whole of the examination, I got Wentworth to stand guard with his loaded shot-gun; and I was very particular that we were never caught there after dusk.

'I decided now to make the experiment of staying a night in the great hall, of course "protected". I spoke about it to Wentworth; but his own attempt had made him so nervous that he begged me to do no such thing. However, I thought it well worth the risk, and I managed in the end to persuade him to be present.

'With this in view, I went to the neighbouring town of Gaunt, and by an arrangement with the Chief Constable I obtained the services of six policemen with their rifles. The arrangement was unofficial, of course, and the men were allowed to volunteer, with a promise of payment.

'When the constables arrived early that evening at the inn, I gave them a good feed; and after that we all set out for the manor. We had four donkeys with us, loaded with fuel and other matters; also two great boar-hounds, which one of the police led. When we reached the house, I set the men to unload the donkeys; whilst Wentworth and I set-to and sealed all the doors, except the main entrance, with tape and wax; for if the doors were really opened, I was going to be sure of the fact. I was going to run no risk of being deceived either by ghostly hallucination, or mesmeric influence.

'By the time that we had sealed the doors, the policemen had unloaded the donkeys, and were waiting, looking about them, curiously. I set two of them to lay a fire in the big grate, and the others I used as I required them. I took one of the boar hounds to the end of the hall furthest from the entrance, and there I drove a staple into the floor, to which I tied the dog with a short tether. Then, round him, I drew upon the floor the figure of a pentacle, in chalk. Outside of the pentacle, I made a circle with garlic. I did exactly the same thing with the other hound; but over in the north-east corner of the big hall, where the two rows of doors make the angle.

'When this was done, I cleared the whole centre of the hall, and put one of the policemen to sweep it; after which I had all my apparatus carried into the cleared space. Then I went over to the main door, and hooked it open, so that the hook would have to be lifted out of the hasp, before the door could be closed.

'After that, I placed lighted candles before each of the

sealed doors, and one in each corner of the big room; and then I lit the fire. When I saw that it was properly alight, I got all the men together, by the pile of things in the centre of the room, and took their pipes from them; for, as the Sigsand MS. has it: "They're must noe lyght come from wythin the barryier". And I was going to make sure.

'I got my tape-measure then, and measured out a circle ninety-nine feet in circumference, and immediately began to chalk it out. The police and Wentworth were tremendously interested, and I took the opportunity to warn them that this was no piece of silly mumming on my part, but done with a definite intention of erecting a barrier between us and any ab-human thing that the night might show to us. I warned them that, as they valued their lives (and more than their lives, it might be), no one must on any account whatever pass beyond the limits of the barrier that I was making.

'After I had drawn the circle, I took a bunch of the garlic, and smudged it right round the chalk circle, a little outside of it. When this was complete, I called for candles from my stock of material. I set the police to lighting them, and as they were lit I took them and sealed them down on to the floor, just along the chalk circle, five inches apart. Each candle measured one inch in diameter, and it took one hundred and ninety-eight candles to complete the circle. I need hardly say that every number and measurement has a significance.

'Then, from candle to candle I took a "gayrd" of human hair, entwining it alternately to the left and to the right, until the circle was completed, and the ends of the final hairs shod with silver, were pressed into the wax of the one hundredth and ninety-eighth candle.

'It had now been dark some time, and I made haste to get the "Defence" complete. To this end I got the men well together, and began to fit the Electric Pentacle right around us, so that the five points of the Defensive Star came just within the Hair-Circle. This did not take me long, and a few minutes later I had connected up the batteries, and the weak blue glare of the intertwining vacuum tubes shone all around us.

'I felt happier then; for this Pentacle is, as you all know, a wonderful "Defence". I have told you before how the idea came to me, after reading Professor Gardor's "Experiments with a Medium". He found that a current, of a certain number of vibrations, *in vacuo*, "insulated" the Medium. It is difficult to suggest an explanation non-technically, and if you are really interested you should read Gardor's lecture on "Astral Vibrations Compared with Matero-involuted Vibrations Below The Six-Billion Limit".

'As I stood up from my work, I could hear outside in the night a constant drip from the laurels, which, as I have said, come right up around the house very thick. By the sound, I knew that a "soft" rain had set in, and there was absolutely no wind, as I could tell by the steady flames of the candles.

'I stood a moment or two, listening, and then one of the men touched my arm, and asked me in a low voice what they should do. By his tone I could tell that he was feeling something of the strangeness of it all; and the other men, including Wentworth, were so quiet that I was afraid they were beginning to get nervy.

'I set-to, then, and arranged them with their backs to one common centre, so that they were sitting flat upon the floor, with their feet radiating outwards. Then, by compass, I laid their legs to the eight chief points, and afterwards I drew a "circle" with chalk round them; and opposite to their feet, I made the Eight Signs of the Saaamaaa Ritual. The eighth place was, of course, empty; but ready for me to occupy at any moment; for I had omitted to make the Sealing Sign to that point, until I had finished all my preparations, and could enter the "Inner Star".

'I took a last look round the great hall, and saw that the two big hounds were lying quietly, with their noses between their paws. The fire was big and cheerful, and the candles before the two rows of doors, burnt steadily, as well as the solitary ones in the corners. Then I went round the little star of men, and warned them not to be frightened whatever happened; but to trust to the "Defence", and to let *nothing* tempt or drive them to cross the Barriers. Also, I told them to watch their movements, and to keep their feet strictly to their places. For the rest, there was to be no shooting, unless I gave the word.

'And now at last, I went to my place, and, sitting down, made the Eighth Sign just beyond my feet. Then I arranged my camera and flashlight handy, and examined my revolver.

'Wentworth sat behind the First Sign, and as the numbering went round reversed, that put him next to me on my left. I asked him, in a low voice, how he felt; and he told me, rather nervous; but that he had confidence in my knowledge, and was resolved to go through with the matter, whatever happened.

'We settled down then to wait. There was no talking, except that, once or twice, the police bent towards one another, and whispered odd remarks concerning the hall … their whispers being queerly audible in the intense silence. But in a while there was not even a word from anyone, and only the monotonous drip, drip of the quiet rain without the great entrance, and the low, dull sound of the fire in the big fireplace.

'It was a queer group that we made sitting there, back to back, with our legs starred outwards; and all around us the strange, weak blue glow of the intertwining Pentacle, and beyond that the brilliant shining of the great ring of lighted candles. Outside of the glare of the candles, the large empty hall looked a little gloomy, by contrast, except where the lights shone before the sealed doors and in the corners; whilst the blaze of the big fire made a good honest mass of flame on the monster hearth. And the feeling of mystery! Can you picture it all?

'It might have been an hour later that it came to me suddenly that I was aware of an extraordinary sense of dreeness, as it were, come into the air of the place. Not the nervous feeling of mystery that had been with us all the time; but a new feeling, as if there were something going to happen any moment.

'Abruptly, there came a slight noise from the east end of the hall, and I felt the start of men move suddenly. "Steady! Keep steady!" I said sharply, and they quietened. I looked up the hall, and saw that the dogs were upon their feet, and staring in an extraordinary fashion towards the great entrance. I turned and stared, also, and felt the men move as they craned their heads to look. Suddenly, the dogs set up a tremendous barking, and I glanced across to them, and found they were still "pointing" for the big doorway. They ceased their noise just as quickly, and seemed to be listening. In the same instant, I heard a faint chink of metal to my left, that set me staring at the hook which held the great door wide. It moved, even as I looked. Some invisible thing was meddling with it. A queer, sickening thrill went through me, and I felt all the men about me, stiffen and go rigid with intensity. I had a certainty of something impending; as it might be the impression of an invisible, but over-whelming, Presence. The hall was full of a queer silence, and not a sound came from the dogs. *Then, I saw the hook slowly raised from out of its hasp, without any visible thing touching it.* A sudden power of movement came to me. I raised my camera, with the flashlight fixed, and snapped it at the door. There came the great blare of the flashlight, and a simultaneous roar of barking from the two dogs.

'The intensity of the flash made all the place seem dark for some moments after, and in that time of darkness, I heard a jingle in the direction of the door, that made me strain to look. The effect of the bright light passed, and I could see clearly again. The great entrance door was being slowly closed. It shut with a sharp snick, and there followed a long silence, broken only by the whimpering of the dogs.

'I turned suddenly, and looked at Wentworth. He was looking at me.

' "Just as it did before," he whispered.

' "Most extraordinary," I said, and he nodded and looked round, nervously.

'The policemen were pretty quiet, and I judged that they

20

were feeling rather worse than Wentworth; though, for that matter, you must not think that I was altogether natural; yet I have seen so much that is extraordinary, that I daresay I can keep my nerves steady longer than most people; at any rate, in that kind of thing.

'I looked over my shoulder at the men, and cautioned them, in a low voice, not to move outside of the Barriers, *whatever happened*; not even though the house should seem to be rocking and about to tumble on them; for I knew well enough what some of the great Forces are capable of doing. Yet, unless it should prove to be one of the cases of the more terrible Saiitii Manifestations, we were almost certain of safety, so long as we kept to our order within the Pentacle.

'Perhaps an hour and a half passed, quietly, except when, once in a way, the dogs would whine distressfully. Presently, however, they ceased even from this, and I could see them lying on the floor with their paws over their noses, in a most peculiar fashion, and shivering visibly. The sight made me feel more serious, as you can understand.

'Suddenly, the candle in the corner furthest from the main door, went out. An instant later, Wentworth jerked my arm, and I saw that a candle before one of the sealed doors had been put out. I held my camera ready. Then, one after another, every candle about the hall was put out, and with such speed and irregularity, that I could never catch one in the actual act of being extinguished. Yet, for all that, I took a flashlight of the hall in general.

'There was a time in which I sat half-blinded by the great glare of the flash, and I blamed myself for not having remembered to bring a pair of smoked goggles, which I have sometimes used at these times. I had felt the men jump, at the sudden light, and I called out loud to them to sit quiet, and to keep their feet exactly to their proper places. My voice, as you can imagine, sounded rather horrid and frightening in the great, empty room, and altogether it was a beastly moment.

'Then, I was able to see again, and I stared round and round the hall; but there was nothing showing unusual; only, of course, it was dark now over in the corners.

'Suddenly, I saw that the great fire was blackening. It was going out visibly, as I looked. If I said that some monstrous, invisible, impossible Force sucked the life from it, I could best explain my impression of the way the light and flame went out of it. It was most extraordinary to watch. In the time that I stared at it, every vestige of fire disappeared, and there was no light outside of the ring of candles around the Pentacle.

'The deliberateness of the thing troubled me more than I can make clear to you. It conveyed to me such a sense of a calm, Deliberate Force present in the hall. The steadfast intention to "make a darkness" was horrible. The *extent* of the Power to affect the Material was now the one constant, anxious questioning in my brain. You can understand?

'Behind me, I heard the policemen moving again, and I knew that they were getting thoroughly frightened. I turned half round, and told them, quietly but plainly, that they were safe only so long as they stayed within the Pentacle, in the position in which I had put them. If they once broke, and went outside of the Barrier, no knowledge of mine could state the full extent or dreadfulness of the danger.

'I steadied them up, by this quiet, straight reminder; but if they had known, as I knew, that there is no *certainty* in any "Protection", they would have suffered a great deal more, and probably have broken the "Defence" and made a mad, foolish run for an impossible safety.

'Another hour passed, after this, in an absolute quietness. I had a sense of awful strain and oppression, as if I were an infinitely insignificant spirit in the company of some invisible, brooding monster of the unseen world, who, as yet, was scarcely conscious of us. I leant across to Wentworth, and asked him in a whisper whether he had a feeling as if Something were in the room. He looked very pale, and his eyes kept always on the move. He glanced just once at me, and nodded; then stared away round the hall again.

'Abruptly, as though a hundred unseen hands had snuffed

them, every candle in the barrier went dead out, and we were left in a darkness that seemed, for a little, absolute; for the light from the Pentacle was too weak and pale to penetrate far across the great hall.

'I tell you, for a moment, I just sat there as though I had been frozen solid. I felt the "creep" go all over me, and seem to stop in my brain. I felt all at once to be given a power of hearing that was far beyond the normal. I could hear my own heart thudding most extraordinarily loud. I began, however, to feel better, after a little; but I simply had not the pluck to move. You can understand?

'Presently, I began to get my courage back. I gripped at my camera and flashlight, and waited. My hands were simply soaked with sweat. I glanced once at Wentworth. I could see him only dimly. His shoulders were hunched a little, his head forward; but though it was motionless, I knew that his eyes were not. It is queer how one knows that sort of thing at times. The police were just as silent. And in this way a while passed.

'A sound broke across the silence. From two sides of the room there came faint noises. I recognised them at once, as the breaking of the sealing-wax. *The sealed doors were opening.* I raised the camera and flashlight, and it was a peculiar mixture of fear and courage that helped me to press the button. As the great belch of light lit up the hall, I felt the men all about me, jump. The darkness fell like a clap of thunder, if you can understand, and seemed tenfold. Yet, in the moment of brightness, I had seen that all the sealed doors were wide open.

'Suddenly, all around us, there sounded a drip, drip, drip, upon the floor of the great hall. I thrilled with a queer, realising emotion, and a sense of a very real and present danger—*imminent*. The "blood-drip" had commenced. And the grim question was now whether the Barriers could save us from whatever had come into the huge room.

'Through some awful minutes the "blood-drip" continued to fall in an increasing rain, and presently some began to fall within the Barriers. I saw several great drops splash and star upon the pale glowing intertwining tubes of the Electric Pentacle; but, strangely enough, I could not trace that any fell among us.

'Beyond the strange horrible noise of the "drip", there was no other sound. And then, abruptly, from the boarhound over in the far corner, there came a terrible yelling howl of agony, followed instantly by a sickening, breaking noise, and an immediate silence. If you have ever, when out shooting, broken a rabbit's neck, you will know the sound that I mean— in miniature! Like lightning, the thought sprang into my brain: *IT has crossed the pentacle*. For you will remember that I had made one about each of the dogs. I thought instantly, with a sick apprehension, of our own Barriers. There was something in the hall with us that had passed the barrier of the pentacle about one of the dogs. In the awful succeeding silence, I positively quivered. And suddenly, one of the men behind me, gave out a scream, like any woman, and bolted for the door. He fumbled, and had it open in a moment. I yelled to the others not to move; but they followed like sheep, and I heard them kick the candles flying, in their panic. One of them stepped on the Electric Pentacle, and smashed it, and there was an utter darkness. In an instant, I realised that I was defenceless against the powers of the Unknown World, and with one savage leap I was out of the useless Barriers, and instantly through the great doorway, and into the night. I believe I yelled with sheer funk.

'The men were a little ahead of me, and I never ceased running, and neither did they. Sometimes, I glanced back over my shoulder; and I kept glancing into the laurels which grew all along the drive. The beastly things kept rustling, rustling in a hollow sort of way, as though something were keeping parallel with me, among them. The rain had stopped, and a dismal little wind kept moaning through the grounds. It was disgusting.

'I caught Wentworth and the police at the lodge gate. We got outside, and ran all the way to the village. We found old Dennis up, waiting for us, and half the villagers to keep him company. He told us that he had known in his "sowl" that we should come back—that is, if we came back at all; which is not a bad rendering of his remark.

'Fortunately, I had brought my camera away from the House—possibly because the strap had happened to be over my head. Yet, I did not go straight away to develop; but sat with the rest in the bar, where we talked for some hours, trying to be coherent about the whole horrible business.

'Later, however, I went up to my room, and proceeded with my photography. I was steadier now, and it was just possible, so I hoped, that the negatives might show something.

'On two of the plates, I found nothing unusual; but on the third, which was the first one that I snapped, I saw something that made me quite excited. I examined it very carefully with a magnifying glass; then I put it to wash, and slipped a pair of rubber half shoes over my boots.

'The negative had shown me something very extraordinary, and I had made up my mind to test the truth of what it seemed to indicate, without losing another moment. It was no use telling anything to Wentworth and the police, until I was certain; and also, I believed that I stood a greater chance to succeed by myself; though, for that matter, I do not suppose anything would have got them up to the Manor again that night.

'I took my revolver, and went quietly downstairs, and into

the dark. The rain had commenced again; but that did not bother me. I walked hard. When I came to the lodge gates, a sudden, queer instinct stopped me from going through, and I climbed the wall into the park. I kept away from the drive, and approached the building through the dismal, dripping laurels. You can imagine how beastly it was. Every time a leaf rustled, I jumped.

'I made my way round to the back of the big House, and got in through a little window which I had taken note of during my search; for, of course, I knew the whole place now from roof to cellars. I went silently up the kitchen stairs, fairly quivering with funk; and at the top, I stepped to the left, and then into a long corridor that opened, through one of the doorways we had sealed, into the big hall. I looked up it, and saw a faint flicker of light away at the end; and I tip-toed silently towards it, holding my revolver ready. As I came near to the open door, I heard men's voices, and then a burst of laughing. I went on, until I could see into the hall. There were several men there, all in a group. They were well dressed, and one, at least, I saw was armed. They were examining my "barriers" against the Supernatural, with a good deal of unkind laughter. I never felt such a fool in my life.

'It was plain to me that they were a gang of men who had made use of the empty Manor, perhaps for years, for some purpose of their own; and now that Wentworth was attempting to take possession, they were acting up to the traditions of the place, with the view of driving him away, and keeping so useful a place still at their disposal. But what they were, I mean whether coiners, thieves, inventors, or what—I could not imagine.

'Presently, they left the Pentacle, and gathered round the living boarhound, which seemed curiously quiet as if it were half-drugged. There was some talk as to whether to let the poor brute live, or not; but finally they decided it would be good policy to kill it. I saw two of them force a twisted loop of rope into its mouth, and the two bights of the loop were brought together at the back of the hound's neck. Then a third man thrust a thick walking-stick through the two loops. The two men with the rope, stooped to hold the dog, so that I could not see what was done; but the poor beast gave a sudden awful howl, and immediately there was a repetition of the uncomfortable breaking sound, I had heard earlier in the night, as you will remember.

'The men stood up, and left the dog lying there—quiet enough now, as you may suppose. For my part, I fully appreciated the calculated remorselessness which had decided upon the animal's death, and the cold determination with which it had been afterwards executed so neatly. I guessed that a man who might get into the "light" of these particular men, would be likely to come to quite as uncomfortable an ending.

'A minute later, one of them called out to the rest that they should "shift the wires". One of the men came towards the doorway of the corridor in which I stood, and I ran quickly back into the darkness of the upper end. I saw the man reach up, and take something from the top of the door, and I heard the slight, ringing jangle of steel-wire.

'When he had gone, I ran back again, and saw the men passing, one after another, through an opening in the stairs, formed by one of the marble steps being raised. When the last man had vanished, the slab that made the step was shut down, and there was not a sign of the secret door. It was the seventh step from the bottom, as I took care to count; and a splendid idea, for it was so solid that it did not ring hollow, even to a fairly heavy hammer, as I found later.

'There is little more to tell. I got out of the House as quickly and quietly as possible, and back to the inn. The police came without any coaxing, when they knew the "ghosts" were normal flesh and blood. We entered the Park and the Manor in the same way that I had done. Yet, when we tried to open the step, we failed, and had finally to smash it. This must have warned the haunters; for when we descended to a secret room which we found at the end of a long and narrow passage in the thickness of the walls, we found no one.

'The police were horribly disgusted, as you can imagine; for they seemed tolerably certain that I had dropped on the meeting-place of a certain "political" club much wanted by the authorities; but for my part, I did not care either way. I had "laid the ghost", as you might say, and that was what I set out to do. I was not particularly afraid of being laughed at by the others; for they had all been thoroughly "taken in"; and in the end, I had scored, without their help.

'We searched right through the secret ways, and found that there was an exit, at the end of a long tunnel, which opened in the side of a well, out in the grounds. The ceiling of the hall was hollow, and reached by a little secret stairway inside of the big staircase. The "blood-drip" was merely coloured water, dropped through the minute crevices of the ornamented ceiling. How the candles and the fire were put out, I do not know; for the haunters certainly did not act quite up to tradition, which held that the lights were put out by the "blood-drip". Perhaps it was too difficult to direct the fluid, without positively squirting it, which might have given the whole thing away. The candles and the fire may possibly have been extinguished by the agency of carbonic acid gas; but how suspended, I have no idea.

'The secret hiding places were, of course, ancient. There was also (did I tell you?) a bell which they had rigged up to ring, when anyone entered the gates at the end of the drive.

If I had not climbed the wall, I should have found nothing for my pains; for the bell would have warned them, had I gone in through the gateway.'

'What was on the negative?' I asked, with much curiosity.

'A picture of the fine wire with which they were grappling for the hook that held the entrance door open. They were doing it from one of the crevices in the ceiling. They had evidently made no preparations for lifting the hook. I suppose they never thought that anyone would make use of it, and so they had to improvise a grapple. The wire was too fine to be seen by the amount of light we had in the hall; but the flashlight "picked it out". Do you see?

'The opening of the inner doors was managed by wires, as you will have guessed, which they unshipped after use, or else I should have found them, when I made my search.

'I think I have now explained everything. The hound was killed, of course, by the men direct. You see, they made the place as dark as possible, first. Of course, if I had managed to take a flashlight just at that instant, the whole secret of the haunting would have been exposed. But Fate just ordered it the other way.'

'And the tramps?' I asked.

'O, you mean the two tramps who were found dead in the Manor,' said Carnacki. 'Well, of course it is impossible to be sure, one way or the other. Perhaps they happened to find out something, and were given a hypodermic. Or it is quite as probable that they had come to the time of their dying, and just died naturally. It is conceivable that a great many tramps had slept in the old house, at one time or another.'

Carnacki stood up, and knocked out his pipe. We rose also, and went for our coats and hats.

'Out you go!' said Carnacki, genially, using the recognised formula. And we went out on to the Embankment, and presently through the darkness to our various houses.